MYRO Arrives in Australia

Belongs to ....

Also available...

Audio CD
Myro, The Smallest Plane In The World

Listen to the songs!

Myro Arrives in Australia
Book 1 from Series 1: Myro Goes to Australia

First published October 2010 by NickRose Ltd
www.nickrose.com
ISBN 978-1-907972-00-3

No part of this publication may be reproduced or transmitted in
any form, or by any means without permission of Nick Rose.
A CIP catalogue record for this book is available from the British Library.
Printed and bound by Butler Tanner & Dennis of Frome, Somerset, England.

Myro's Team
Concept and Story: Nick Rose
Illustrations and Branding: Lucy Corrina Bourn
Designer: Sue Mason
Writer: Fiona Veitch Smith
Editor: Mary O'Riordan
Editorial Consultant: Samantha Mackintosh
Australian Consultant: Jane Massam
3D Consultancy: Jon Stuart and Sean Frisby
Project Management: Nick Rose
Continue the fun at www.myro.com

nr.
nickrose ltd

MYRO
Arrives in
AUSTRALIA

Nick Rose

Myro the microlight is the smallest plane in the world . . .

He loves to fly!

"I'm Myro the microliiiiiiiight!" yelled the tiny aircraft, zoooming high in the sky. "Watch out, Australia, here I come!"

Myro took off before the cargo ship had even docked. It had taken forever to get here from the UK and he was desperate to stretch his wings.

"Oi!" called Rolo the Routemaster. "Come down, Myro! You don't have a permit to fly yet."

Myro's wing was taken off and he was wheeled
onto a trailer behind the bus.

The two friends drove from Sydney Harbour, out of the city,
up the East Coast . . .

. . . through the bush and
past the vineyards . . .

. . . until they reached Myro's new home, at the Flying Club
in the Hunter Valley.

"I'm sure you'll love living here, Myro," said Rolo, turning to leave.

"*Wait!*" cried the little microlight. "Where are you going?"

"I'm off to Sydney," said Rolo. "Don't worry! I'll be back in a few days."

Just then, a lady walked over.
"G'day, Myro, welcome to Australia!" she said.
"I'm Madge the manager and I'm in charge
of the Flying Club."

"And I'm Michael, your new pilot," said a
friendly man. "Let's get your wing back on
so you can meet your new mates."

With his wing on, Myro felt
ready for anything.

"You'll be living with Gigi, Hyli and Cylo,"
said Madge, going over to Myro's new hangar.
Inside were three aircraft, impatient to meet him.

"G'day, everyone," said Myro in his best
Australian accent, and they all laughed.

"See, he's already speaking our language!"
said Hyli the helicopter.

"Huh! Let's see how well he does in the sky,"
huffed Gigi the gyrocopter.

"Don't mind her," said Cylo the Cessna
with a friendly whir of his yellow propeller.
"She's not usually so grumpy."

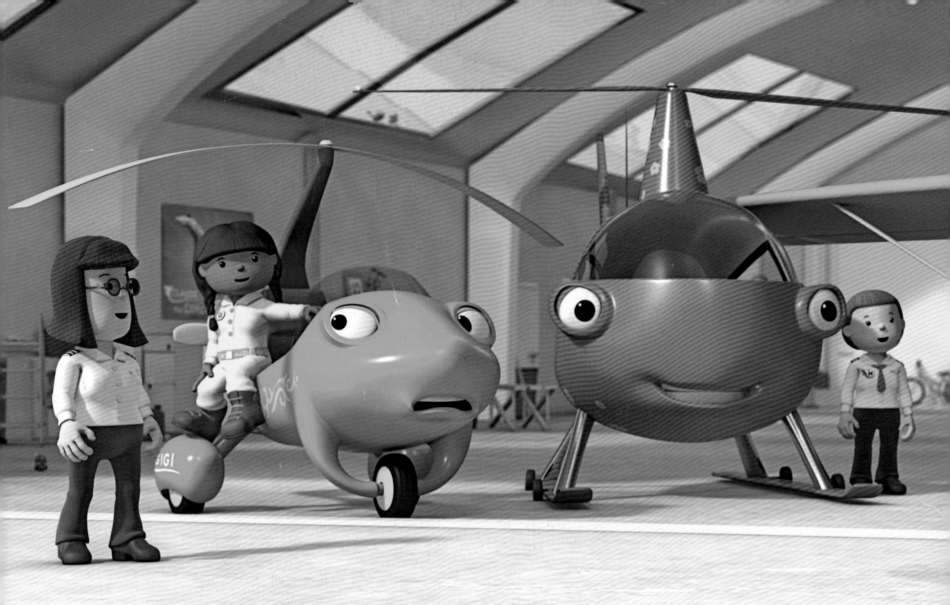

"Why don't you show Gigi how well you can fly, Myro?"
said Madge. "You can help her muster sheep."

"I can do it myself," said Gigi.

"It will be fun to fly with Myro," said Madge firmly.

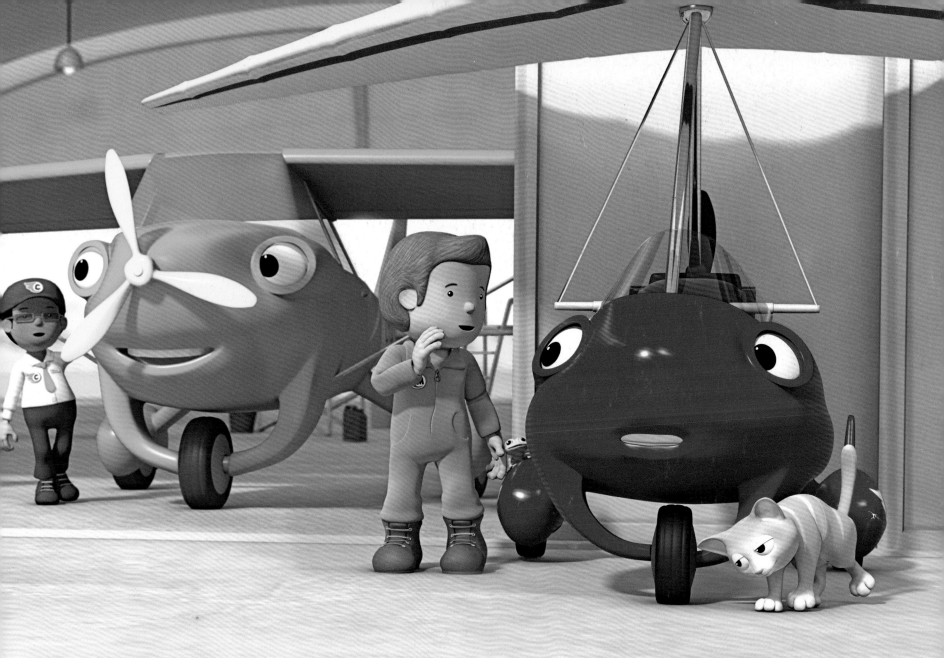

Myro had the feeling Gigi wasn't so keen on having him around.

"Don't worry," whispered Michael. "She's only upset because she's not the smallest in the hangar any more."

Gigi and Myro were soon flying side by
side over scrubby fields, winding rivers
and little hills covered in bush.

Far below him, Myro could see strange animals bouncing
along on their back legs.

"*Wow!*" he said.

"Never seen kangaroos before?" asked Gigi.

"No," said Myro.

"You only get them here in Australia,"
said the gyrocopter, and she picked up speed.

"Hey, wait for me!" said Myro,
whirring quickly after her.

When they got to the farm, the sheep
were easy to find.

"Watch this!" yelled Gigi, and she swooped low,
mustering the woolly animals like a sheep dog.

"Not bad flying!" said Myro.

"Not bad?" asked Gigi. "Let's see if you can do better."

But before Myro could
zoom down he spotted something.

"Look over there! There's a sheep
stuck in a fence!"

"Get your pilot to radio the farmer," bossed
Gigi. "There's nothing we can do – no one can
land in the paddock with all those cows over there."

"Hang on! Give me a chance!" shouted Myro.

And with a splutter and a buzz from his propeller, he mustered the cows to one side, just as Gigi had done with the sheep.

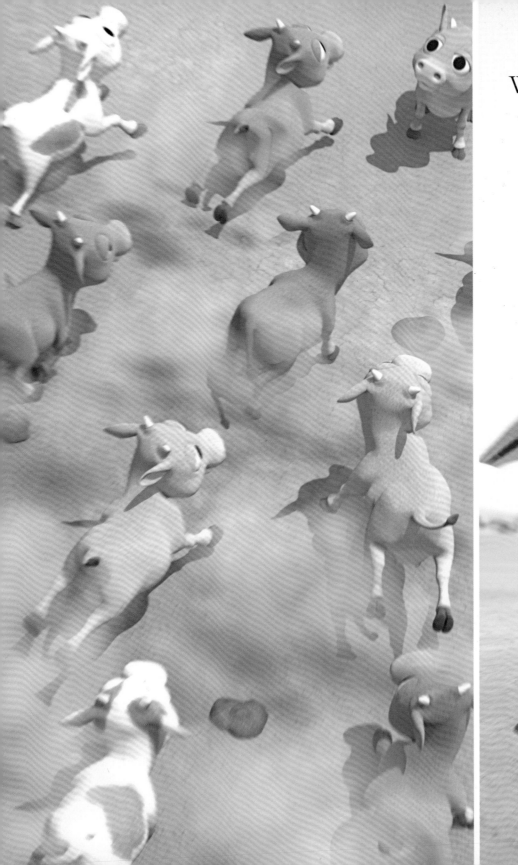

When the paddock was clear, the little microlight zoooomed in to land.

"Yuk!" yelled Myro, suddenly seeing cow pats *everywhere!* He swerved wildly, dodging the poos all the way until …

Splat!

"Hey! You can really fly!" laughed Gigi, landing beside Myro.

"Thank you!" grinned Myro.

Gigi winked. "You could work on the driving skills,
though – you hit a lot of smelly poo on the way!"

They laughed together as their pilots untangled the sheep
from the fence. It was puffing and panting like crazy.

"Strewth!" exclaimed Michael. "I think this sheep is about to have a baby!"

"Hurry, Michael!" cried Myro as his pilot strapped the mother-to-be into the back seat. "There'll be no room to take off if those cows keep coming closer!"

"Let's go!" yelled Gigi.

Myro and Gigi raced down the paddock

‑ *splat!* splat! splat! through the poo –

taking off not a moment too soon as Myro's wheels
just clipped the tip of a huge bull's horns.

A few minutes later they landed on the little airstrip at the farm.

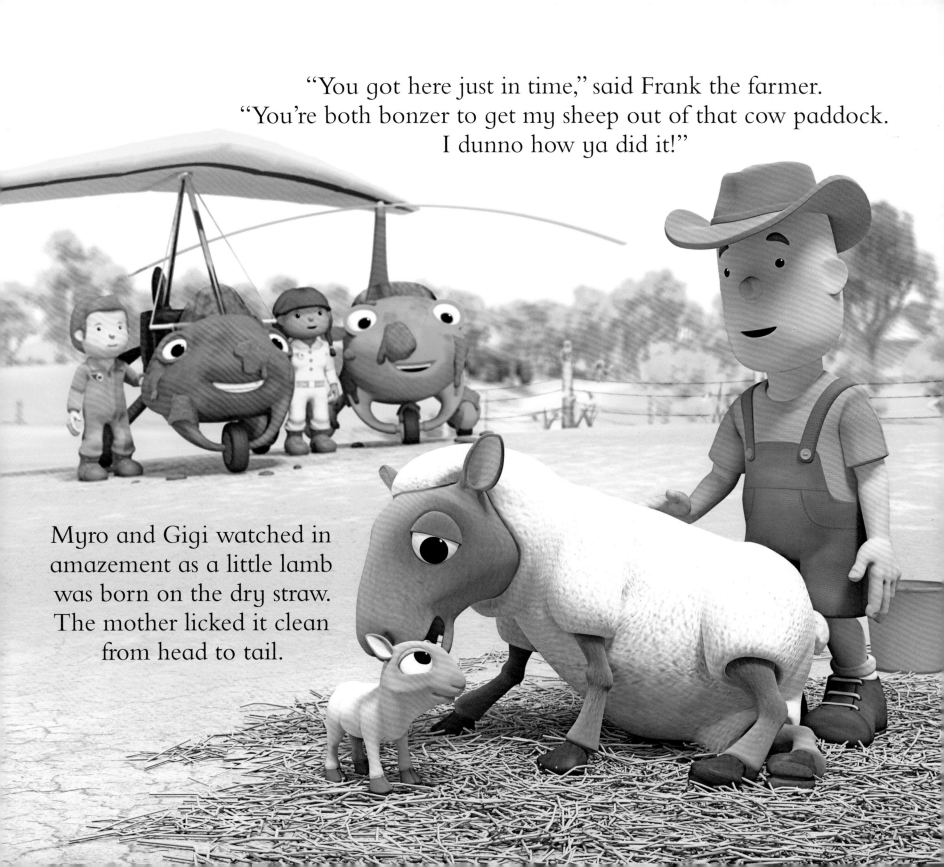

"You got here just in time," said Frank the farmer.
"You're both bonzer to get my sheep out of that cow paddock.
I dunno how ya did it!"

Myro and Gigi watched in
amazement as a little lamb
was born on the dry straw.
The mother licked it clean
from head to tail.

When Myro and Gigi landed back at the Flying Club,
Hyli and Cylo were waiting for them.

"Congrats, mate!" said Cylo.
"Heard you can fly like a jet fighter!"

"Come on, Myro," said Hyli. "We've got
a surprise for you."

"Whoa!" said Madge loudly.

"You're going to need a hose down before entering your hangar. You two smell like a cow's bum!"

"SURPRISE!"
yelled everybody, when Myro and
Gigi taxied into the hangar at last.

Myro's new home was filled with streamers and balloons!

"Come on in!" grinned Michael. "It's your
Welcome to Australia party."

"Thanks, guys," said Myro, smiling happily.
"I think I'm going to like living Down Under!"